This book was inspired by and is dedicated to my glorious little boy,
Declan.
May you continue to build with great passion.
Like all of YOUR creations, you are truly an amazing work of art.

And to our lost little kitty cat, Pumpkin, and all of the kitty cats who have been part of our family over
the years, we love you and are forever
grateful to you for the

contribution you've made to our happiness and well being.

Declan's Marbles and the Lost Tabby Cat

by Calleen Coorough
Illustrated by Eric Famanas

Declan lived on beautiful Camano Island with his mom and his kitty cats. He loved kitty cats!

Declan also loved to build things. He was good at it too --
really good at it.

When he was just a little guy, he would
spend the entire day building things.

His most favorite thing to build was the
perfect marble run.

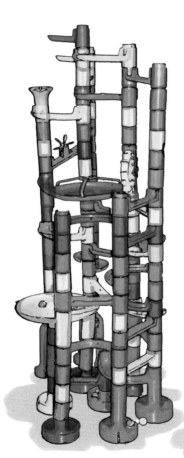

All his marble runs were perfect really.
The big ones were perfect.
The little ones were perfect.
The fast ones were perfect.
The slow ones where the marbles took their time
traveling down a tornado twisty
were SUPER perfect.

3

Declan started building marble runs
when he was about 3 years old.

For every birthday and every
Christmas, Declan would ask
for another marble run toy
to add to his collection.

"I love marble runs!"
He would say.

By age 6, he had 13 different marble run toys. He had block & roll marble runs, classic marble runs, marble runs with gears and bumpity bumps.
He also had marble runs with battery-operated elevators and spinners.

From these, he could build an endless number of marble runs.

His Grandpa Bob even made him a one-of-a-kind wooden marble run complete with hippo, giraffe and a crocodile that spurt marbles out its mouth.

When Declan played with his marbles, his imagination went wild. Over and over again, he would say, "Mom, watch my amazing marble run!"

Through the curve, over the bumpity bump, down the twisty, across the slide, and into the snake, Declan's marbles raced this way and that way, dumping out into a bucket.

"Sometimes first is last and last is first."
He would say, as he loaded an entire handful
of marbles into a marble run with three tornado
twisties.

"I'm gonna race these marbles! Now I'll do a super marble race. Whoever wins gets to be king of marble races."

"It's blue! It's blue! Blue is first, green is second, yellow is third, red is fourth, orange is fifth and the cat eye marble is last."

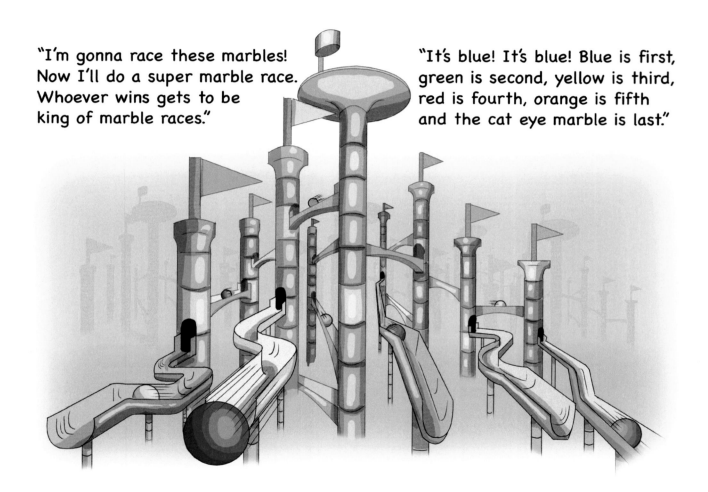

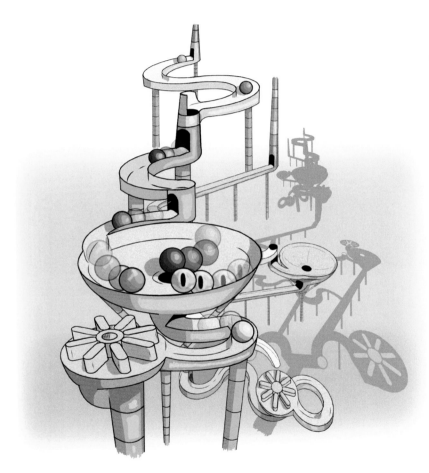

You never knew the outcome once a marble hit a tornado twisty.

Sometimes the first marble into the tornado twisty was the last one out.

Tornado twisties were always full of surprises.

It took two people to build a marble run down the stairs. One person to hold the pieces steady and the other to add on.

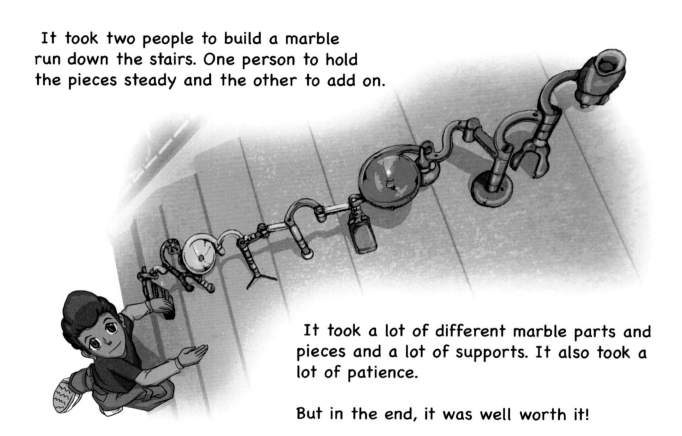

It took a lot of different marble parts and pieces and a lot of supports. It also took a lot of patience.

But in the end, it was well worth it!

"Let's add dominoes." Declan would say.

Down the marbles race, knocking over a stack of dominoes at the end of the run.

"Oh!!! Look at that!!!"
Declan would exclaim.

Sometimes the marbles get going so fast they fly out of the marble run and across the floor.

Runaway Marbles!!!!!

That's when the kittens would come out to play. Pumpkin and Faith get in the game, batting and chasing marbles through the house and under the refrigerator.

Of all Declan's kitty cats, and he had a lot of kitty cats, Pumpkin loved to play marbles the most. As soon as he heard Declan drop a marble in the run, out he would come to watch the marbles go down and around and in and out.

It was fascinating and so much fun when one of the marbles escaped.

15

One day, Declan and his mom loaded the kitty cats into the car
to take them to the vet. Pumpkin was very scared.

He didn't understand what was happening. He tried and tried to get out
of his carrier.

The vet's office was about 15 minutes from their house.
By the time they arrived, Pumpkin was so scared that
he broke free of his carrier and raced across the parking
lot to a huge wooded area filled with blackberry bushes.

Declan and his mom ran after Pumpkin, but he was too fast.
Pumpkin was gone and the brush was too thick.
Declan and his mom called and called for Pumpkin,
but he didn't appear.

A crowd began to form as others who had seen Pumpkin bolt from his carrier into the woods offered to help.

Workers rushed out from the vet's office and surrounding businesses.

Everybody wanted to find Pumpkin!!!

Declan and his mom looked and looked
and looked for Pumpkin, but they couldn't
find him. Finally, night came. Tired and
hungry they went home in tears.

At sunrise, they would return to look
for Pumpkin again.

For several weeks, Declan and his mom returned to look for Pumpkin.

They hung flyers with Pumpkin's picture and description.

They posted information to websites for missing pets.

They even secured the help of delivery people and the police hoping someone would see Pumpkin and they would get their beloved kitty cat back again.

They had many calls from people
who were sure they had found Pumpkin.
Each time they got their hopes up, but
their hearts quickly fell with disappointment.
None of the cats was Pumpkin.

Pumpkin was nowhere to be found.

Each night they went to bed hoping that Pumpkin would find his way home and that they would wake up to find him in one of his favorite spots.

But each morning they awoke to the same aching heart.

Their beloved kitty cat was gone.

Declan and his mom were losing hope.
They were worried about Pumpkin's well being.
Was he alive?
Was he scared?
Was he cold?
Was he hungry?
Would they ever see him again?

Suddenly, Declan had an idea!!!!
"Mom, I know what to do to get Pumpkin back. We'll build a marble
run and take it to the blackberry bramble where we lost Pumpkin.
When he hears it, he'll know it's us and he'll come running out to play!"

So Declan set out to build the most
amazing marble run ever. It had
curves, bumpity bumps, twisties, slides,
snakes, and a big bucket at the end.

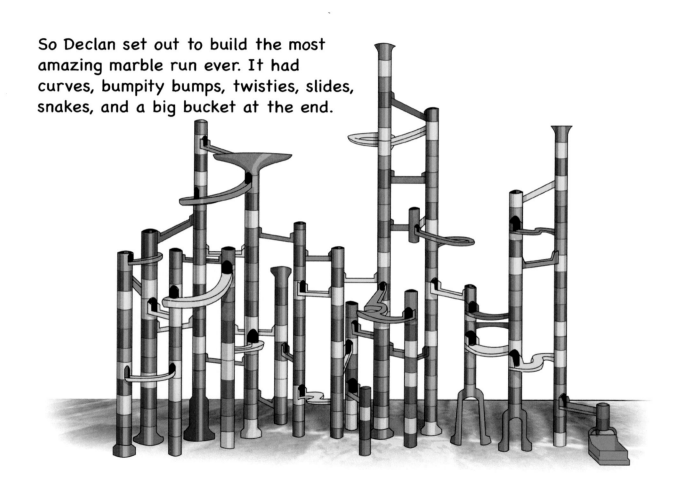

Very carefully, Declan and his mom loaded the marble run into the car and headed over to the blackberry bramble where they last saw Pumpkin.

The marble run was their last hope.

Declan loaded the blue marble into the marble run. Down it went making the familiar clickety-clack tune they hoped Pumpkin would remember.

They waited..., nothing.

Declan tried again. He loaded the green, yellow, red and orange marbles, but no Pumpkin.

Last try. The cat eye marble.
Declan dropped it in.
Down it went...

Through the curve, over the bumpity bump, down the twisty, across the slide, into the snake and out into the bucket with a final loud "CLANG!" But it didn't stop in the bucket. This marble was going so hard and so fast that it jumped out of the bucket and skated to the edge of the blackberry bushes where they had last seen Pumpkin.

They waited....
Then, they heard a rustle from the blackberry bramble.
Could it be Pumpkin?

From beneath the blackberry bramble where the cat eye marble rested, a skinny, matted, brown tabby cat emerged.

It was Pumpkin!!!

Tears of joy streaming down their faces,
Declan and his mom scooped up a purring Pumpkin and took him home.

The marble run worked!! At last,
they had found their beloved kitty cat.

Calleen Coorough is a published author and teacher. She loves everything "feline" and enjoys living on beautiful Camano Island in Washington State with her son, Declan. When she's not in front of her computer, you can find Calleen playing with her kitty cats, hanging out with her son, or hiking a nearby trail.

Eric Famanas is a veteran of the United States Navy and an aspiring software engineer in Cambridge, United Kingdom. When taking a break from his work and studies, he enjoys practicing his character illustrations. Whenever he has a moment, Eric will take some time to watch anime or play video games with his family.

Made in the USA
Lexington, KY
09 October 2017